Postman P
and the
Barometer

Story by John Cunliffe
Pictures by Ray Mutimer
Based on the TV Special designed by Ivor Wood

Little Hippo

Look out for more Postman Pat and Jess adventures in
Postman Pat and the Toy Soldiers
Postman Pat takes the Bus
Postman Pat and the Tuba

Scholastic Children's Books,
Commonwealth House, 1-19 New Oxford Street,
London WC1A 1NU, UK
a division of Scholastic Ltd

London ~ New York ~ Toronto ~ Sydney ~ Auckland

First published by Scholastic Ltd, 1994

This edition published by Little Hippo, an imprint of Scholastic Ltd, 1998

Text copyright © John Cunliffe, 1994
Illustrations copyright © Scholastic Ltd & Woodland Animations Ltd, 1994

ISBN 0 590 19816 5

Printed by Proost, Belgium

"It's time we had some new wallpaper," said Sara, one gloomy winter day.

"I'll get two dozen rolls from Ted," said Pat.

"You won't," said Sara. "We'll all go to Pencaster to pick something really smart. It'll be a nice day out."

So that is what they did.

3

It took a long time.

Julian liked the one with balloons on it.

Pat liked the one with cats and flowers.

Sara liked what she said was a 'William Morris' one, with birds and flowers on it.

"I thought he made cars," said Pat.

"Don't be silly," said Sara. "That was another Morris. We'll have this one. It's just right for our house."

"It'll take some putting up," said Pat. "With a pattern like that."

"You'll manage," said Sara.

Pat did manage, on his Saturday off, but it was hard work.

"What about the barometer?" he said, when he came to paper the sitting-room.

"It will have to come down," said Sara.

"But ..." said Pat.

"The barometer's not so bad," said Sara, "but look at that old hook."

"But," said Pat, "I look at it every morning to see what the weather's going to be."

"The hook?" said Sara.

"No," said Pat, "the *barometer*."

"You could put it somewhere else," said Julian.

"Yes," said Sara, "it does seem a pity to spoil the nice new paper with that rusty old hook."

"I'll see what I can do," said Pat, sighing. "I think there's a hook in the bathroom."

Pat hung the barometer in the bathroom.

On Monday morning, he tapped it to see what the weather would be. Its finger was between RAIN and STORM.

"It's going to be a rough day," said Pat.

He went out in his wellingtons, scarf, and raincoat, and took his biggest umbrella. The sun shone all day! He was too hot, and Jess tore the umbrella with his claws.

"I can't understand it," said Pat. "Granny's old barometer never used to be wrong about the weather."

"You could put it in the kitchen," said Sara on Tuesday. "There's a spare hook by the stove."

Pat hung the barometer in the kitchen.

On Wednesday, he tapped it to see what the weather would be. Its finger pointed to SET FAIR.

"It's going to be a lovely sunny day," said Pat.

He went out without a coat, and he wore his sandals.

It poured with rain all day, and he got soaked. It was cold, too.

"I can't understand it," said Pat. "Granny's old barometer never used to be wrong about the weather."

"You could put it at the foot of our stairs," said Sara on Thursday. "There's a spare hook by the coat-hooks."

Pat hung the barometer behind the front door, at the foot of the stairs. There were quite a few visitors on that day. It was a draughty spot.

On Friday, he tapped it to see what the weather would be. Its finger pointed to CHANGEABLE.

"That means wind," said Pat, "and plenty of it. I'll take young Julian up the hill to fly his kites after school."

Julian spent a lot of time getting his kites ready. When Pat came home they took them up the hill. There was no wind at all, and the kites would not fly.

"Oh dear," said Pat, "there must be something wrong with that barometer. It never used to be like that."

On Saturday, it was Pat's day off, and they went shopping again in Pencaster. Julian wanted a flask to take on the school fell-walk.

Sara said, "I don't know what *I* want, but I'll just pop into Ted's antique-shop to see if he has anything new."

"He doesn't sell new things," said Pat.

"I know, silly," said Sara, "you know well enough what I mean. Old and new at the same time."

She found just the thing.
"A hook," said Pat.
"A *Victorian* hook," said Sara.
"What use is that?" said Julian.
"It's just the thing..." said Sara, "to hang that barometer on."
"It's already on a hook," said Pat.
"In the hall," said Julian.
"It won't do there," said Sara. "It could go back."
"Back?" said Pat.

"Where it's always been, since granny put it up. It'll be better there."

"But," said Pat, "you said we couldn't..."

"I know," said Sara, "but this is different. It's *Victorian*. It'll go with the new wallpaper."

"Go?"

"Yes. It'll match it. It's a Victorian hook; like the barometer itself. It will look a treat."

They bought the Victorian hook, and the modern flask, then went round the market for the fruit and vegetables.

By Monday morning, the barometer was back in its usual place on its new-old Victorian hook.

"It completes the room," said Sara.

Pat tapped the barometer.

"It says SNOW," he said.

"Never in this world," said Sara. "Look out of the window. There's not a cloud in the sky."

"Snow?" said Julian. "Great!"

"What about your school fell-walk!" said Sara.

"Great!" said Julian. "I'll take some extra sandwiches, and my new flask."

"It won't snow," said Sara. "That barometer's gone silly. It was wrong all last week."

All the same, Julian took his flask and extra sandwiches, and Pat put a shovel and a bag of sand and salt in his van.

"Just in case," they both said.

Pat was on his way with the letters. Everywhere he went, he told people that snow was on the way.

"Snow?" said Mrs Goggins. "The radio said it would be cold but fine. Just look what Jess's done to my ball of string! More like a whirlwind, I'd say!"

"Snow?" said Miss Hubbard. "We'll not be seeing snow this side of Christmas!"

"Snow?" said Doctor Gilbertson. "I go by the met-office...more scientific...they have computers and satellites; better than your barometer nowadays, Pat."

"Snow?" said Alf. "The man in the paper said it was set fine for two weeks."

"Oh, dear," said Pat to Jess. "No-one believes in my old barometer any more."

No-one did, wherever Pat went that day.

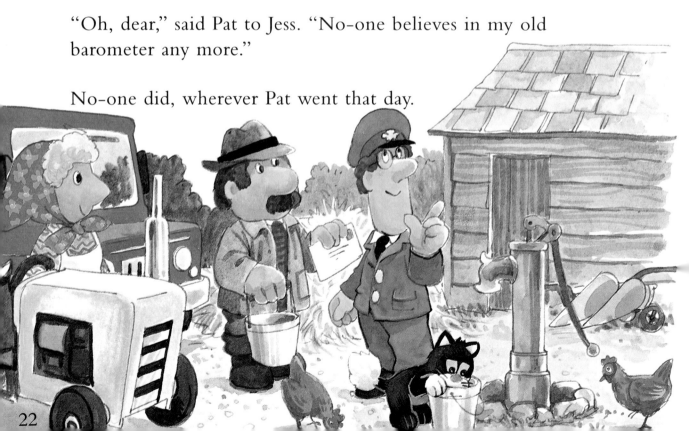

When big flakes of snow began dropping out of the sky, Pat was as surprised as everyone else. They came faster and faster, and soon began to fill up the fields and the roads.

"We'll be blocked in if this goes on," said Granny Dryden.

When Pat arrived at the village school, all was quiet. Where were all the children, and Mr Pringle? Then Pat remembered.

"They've gone on the fell-walk! Off into the hills with a picnic. Oh, Jess, what if they get lost in the snow?"

A door banged, and there were Sara and Ted.

"Oh, Pat!" said Sara. "It looks as if the old barometer was right this time. Ted brought me over in the lorry."

"Sara can stay here and keep warm with the other mums," said Ted, "and we'll go and look for the children. We don't want them getting stuck for the night in this snow. Now, then, no need to panic. Just get that stove stoked up, and keep nice and warm."

Pat brought the shovel and the bag of sand and salt from his van. Ted's lorry hadn't gone far when they got stuck on a slippery patch on the hill near Thompson Ground.

"That always was a bad bit," said Ted. "That sand's a good idea."

Ted dug the snow out, and Pat scattered the sand and salt under the wheels. The lorry was soon on the move again.

"A *very* good idea," said Ted.

On they went, with the snow getting deeper and deeper.
And then the engine started cutting out.

"It's got wet from all this snow," said Ted. "I'll have to stop and
dry the plugs."

It was very quiet when they stopped.
"Listen!" said Pat. "Can you hear?"
"What?" said Ted.
"Singing...!"
"Singing?"
"Coming from over there," said Pat. "I think I know where they are. I'll go and look..."

And that was how Pat and Ted found Mr Pringle and all the children, sheltering from the snow-storm in a barn, and rescued them, and brought them home safely in the end.

"Ooh, we had a smashing time," said Julian. "That picnic was really really good. My sandwiches tasted *sensational*, and my flask was magic."

"It was a pity," said Sara, "that Mr Pringle twisted his ankle."

"Doctor Gilbertson will soon put him to rights," said Pat. "And the children know their first-aid. She says what they did was all for the best."

They all went home to have a good supper and a hot bath. Best of all was to be tucked up in their warm beds, with two hot-water bottles each. Julian says that Pat had three hot-water bottles that night, but he didn't tell anyone; well, not until a long time afterwards.